SERVANT OF LIGHT

ROBERT DALE

SERVANT OF LIGHT
Copyright © 2025 by Robert Dale

Scripture quotations are taken from the Holy Bible, King James Version, which is in the public domain.

ISBN: 978-1-4866-2698-4
eBook ISBN: 978-1-4866-2699-1

Word Alive Press
119 De Baets Street Winnipeg, MB R2J 3R9
www.wordalivepress.ca

WORD ALIVE
—P R E S S—

Cataloguing in Publication information can be obtained from Library and Archives Canada.

To my lovely wife Alice:
I waited decades to meet you, and while
that was hard, you were worth the wait.
I love you.
—Bob

What man of you, having an hundred sheep, if he lose one of them, doth not leave the ninety and nine in the wilderness, and go after that which is lost, until he find it? And when he hath found it, he layeth it on his shoulders, rejoicing. And when he cometh home, he calleth together his friends and neighbours, saying unto them, Rejoice with me; for I have found my sheep which was lost. (Luke 15:4–6)

ONE
July 18, 1997

hree preteen boys rode their bicycles down the streets of Dalberton. They were deliriously happy as only young people can be, laughing and singing to each other. The boys were going home after the best night of their lives. They'd just attended an evening youth service at Harmony Christian Fellowship Church, and two of them had become Christians!

Al Mitchell and Red Harnett had trusted Jesus as their Lord and Saviour this night. They both felt such joy and peace that they couldn't stay silent. They were singing with Jeremy Parker, the boy who'd invited them to the church.

"He is the way, He is the truth, He is the liiiiife, that's Jesus!

"You are the way, you are the truth, you are the liiiiife, Lord Jesus!

"He is the way, He is the truth, He is the liiiiife, my Jesus!"

They'd learned the song at the church, and they loved it. The three boys were very close in age—in fact, their birthdays all fell within weeks of each other.

Red and Al had lived their entire lives in Dalberton and had known each other since the first day of school. Jeremy had moved there just over two years ago and had become instant friends with the other two boys. The three had been inseparable since the day they met.

Jeremy came from a strong Christian home and had told the other boys about Jesus very soon after meeting them. Red and Al had never gone to church, so they were curious and quickly agreed to go to the youth night with him. Now they themselves had trusted Jesus, and they weren't afraid to tell it to the world.

Jeremy had never felt so happy. He wanted to share the love of Jesus with as many as he could, and the fact that his two best friends were now Christians was the best feeling in the world.

As they rode along, the chain slipped off of the gears on Jeremy's bicycle for the third time.

"Aw man, not again!" he exclaimed, letting the other two know it had happened once more.

"You gotta get a new bike," Al told him.

"Yeah, that one's had the biscuit," Red agreed.

"I know, but I don't have enough money saved up yet.

The bike I want is $200, and I only have $150!" Jeremy explained. He reset the chain and the three carried on towards home.

They were singing again as they turned onto the street they all called home. Al and Red were so into the song that they didn't notice when the chain again slipped off of the sprocket on Jeremy's bike. They carried on for another minute before they realized their friend wasn't there. Turning back, they saw that he was almost a block away, so they began to ride towards him.

At that moment, a car turned onto the street and came their way, veering left and right. Jeremy was unaware of the vehicle as he knelt to align the chain on the front gear yet again. His friends watched in horror as the careening car crashed directly into him! The collision killed the young boy instantly, and the driver made no indication that he'd even noticed the impact.

An unseen dark being chuckled. "That'll teach the young preacher. Now I'll tear these other two apart!"

Two

Present Day

Al Mitchell awoke in a sweat, breathing heavily and shaking. *Not again. I haven't had that dream in years. Why now?* The dream was the recollection—reliving, really—of the night he had become a Christian and Jeremy had died in front of him. It had haunted him for years afterwards, causing him to awake drenched in sweat, shaking and panting, as it had on this night. He knew the answer to his outspoken question even as he asked it.

Red.

His lone friend who'd shared the experience with him had suffered greatly for years as well. The long-haired red-headed boy had dealt with the horror of that night very differently than Al had. Red's way of dealing with it at first was by acting out—being difficult in class and with elders. Soon it escalated to fighting in the schoolyard with others, and he even took a few shots at the male teachers. It only got worse from there, and by the time he turned fifteen, he was sent to juvenile hall.

The threatened shooting in the hospital the previous night had stirred up all of these memories in Al. He knew that Jesus was calling out to him, that He wanted him to come back to Him. The experienced police sergeant recognized that he was at a fork in his life-road. A decision had to be made, and he was more afraid than he'd ever been—except for that night.

"Jesus," he began, unsure of what to say, "Lord, I know you've been trying to get my attention for a long time now. I can't lie to you or pretend about this. I'm afraid to trust you again. The night Jeremy—" A sob caused him to pause. "The night Jeremy was killed hurt me so badly, Lord, so badly. I never understood why you let him die, and I still don't. He was such a great guy, Lord Jesus. He was the best, just like Red. I want to trust you again; I can't keep going on without you. Please come back into my life, Lord Jesus. I'm sorry that I've resisted you for so many years." He remembered the way Jeremy always ended his prayers. "In Jesus' name. Amen."

He went into the bathroom to wash the tear stains off his face. But when he looked into the mirror, he didn't see his own reflection but an ancient Roman soldier! Gasping in shock, he staggered back a half-step, watching in utter confusion as the soldier in the mirror moved in exact time with him.

What is happening? was all he could think.

THREE
July 18, 1997

Al and Red were horrified at the sight of the car impacting Jeremy. It had thrown him into the air, and he'd landed with a sickening thud. After watching the driver carry on with no recognition that he had hit Jeremy, both boys went into action.

"Go for help—you're the fastest rider!" Al instructed Red.

Red sped down the road as fast as his legs would take him while Al knelt next to their friend.

The young Jeremy Parker was already gone, at only twelve years of age. Al could see this, and he wept for his friend. "Jesus, why?" he cried out as people from houses came running to the street. Adults were there now and were trying to comfort him. They told him to come away from Jeremy's body, but he wouldn't leave his friend. Red soon returned with all three of the boys' parents.

Jeremy's parents sobbed openly when they saw their son, and at this point Al moved away from the body. Red stood next to him and they clung together, not knowing how to feel or even what to say.

Sirens announced the coming emergency crew.

A friendly-looking officer walked up to the two boys and introduced himself as Sergeant Whitaker. He explained that he knew the boys were hurting and upset, but he needed to ask them some questions. The boys just nodded that they understood, and the kind officer went on.

"Tell me what happened in your own words. Try to remember as much as you can, ok?"

"Jeremy's chain kept falling off, so he'd stopped to fix it again. This car turned onto the street way down at the end and it was weaving back and forth."

"We were yelling for Jeremy to watch out, but he didn't hear us!" Red put in.

"Ok, then what happened?"

"The guy seemed like he was aiming at Jeremy, and then …" Al couldn't continue and began to sob again.

"He hit Jeremy so hard that he flew into the air." Now Red broke down.

"Did he slow down or stop after he hit Jeremy?"

"Not at all. It was like he didn't care!" Red had regained his composure and was now just angry.

"Maybe he didn't know he'd hit Jeremy," the sergeant suggested.

"No way! Jeremy flew up in the air right in front of him!"

"I see. Did you get a good look at the car or the driver?"

Al came back into the conversation. "The car was big and black, but I don't know what kind it was. I did see some of the license plate, though."

"Ok, what part did you see?"

"Just the first three digits—547. I couldn't see the rest."

"Good, that's really good. Did you see the driver?"

"I saw him, but … he was weird," Red said.

"Weird how?"

"I couldn't see him clearly; it was like the inside of the car was dark."

"Ok … that is weird, but I'll look into it. Well, I think that's enough, boys. You've been great, thank you. If you think of anything else or you just want to talk, you can call me anytime."

Al really liked this man, and for the first time in his life he thought that police work might be for him.

The sergeant gave the boys and their parents grief counsellors' cards and his own personal and work phone numbers. The families went to their respective homes to try to deal with the devastating event.

The dark figure was laughing out loud, hidden from physical sight.

FOUR
Present Day

Al had called Ben Parsons, knowing that he had become a Christian less than two years ago. Al had been the officer on duty when Ben's wife was killed, and they'd kept in touch afterwards. He simply said that he needed to talk to him and Kranti Kholi about Sammy Silverton. It was a partial truth, because he also wanted to ask them about this strange reflection he'd seen in his mirror.

An hour later, Ben and Kranti explained how the spiritual side of life worked. They showed him how to shift from the physical view of the world to the spiritual and back. He even learned that we all have a position in the army of God, and his was called a "Protector."

He liked that.

He thanked the men for their help and told them he planned to be at the next Sunday service. He got back into Old Blue, as he called it—the classic muscle-car he'd owned for the past fourteen years. It had chrome wheels, dual exhaust, a big V8 engine, and beautiful blue paint.

Driving Old Blue had been therapeutic for him over the years. The rumble of the engine, the feel of the road, and the sense of freedom always calmed him. He knew that's how Red felt about Scarlett, his custom chopper. Scarlett was painted in several shades of red with an airbrushed picture of a seductive woman on the tank top. Red had owned Scarlett for as long as Al had owned Old Blue.

Red.

He knew he needed to talk to him, but he wasn't sure how to breach the subject of his returning to the Lord. Red had never healed from Jeremy's death, and the fact was, neither had Al—until now. When he thought about Jeremy now, he didn't experience the same sadness and devastation. He actually began to feel the joy of that night before Jeremy had died.

Without realizing it, he began to sing an old song from his past.

"He is the way, He is the truth, He is the liiiiife, that's Jesus!"

That old dark enemy that had watched Jeremy die years ago was watching again. And it was becoming angry.

FIVE

July 25, 1997

◆

Jeremy's funeral took place in a peaceful part of the Dalberton Cemetery. Al and Red stood next to each other, watching as the small casket was lowered into the ground. They knew it was just their friend's body in the casket, but they still couldn't believe he was gone.

Both of the boys were remembering the many times they'd hung out with Jeremy. They'd done everything together: baseball, hiking, riding their bikes, swimming. They'd even had sleepovers at each other's homes. Even though they'd only met two short years ago, they felt like they'd known him all of their lives.

The service was over and people were invited to the Parkers' home for food and a time of remembrance. Al and Red travelled with their respective parents to Jeremy's house. When they got there, Al walked up to Red.

"I guess we have to go inside." He sighed heavily. This was the hard part.

"I can't, Al. I just can't," Red stated flatly. And with that, he ran off towards his own home.

Al watched as his friend bolted away down the street. His mother put a comforting hand on his shoulder.

"Let him go, Allen. He needs time."

Al just nodded with tears on his face. He knew she was right, but he felt more alone now than ever.

More unheard laughter echoed across the spiritual realm at that moment.

six
Present Day

Al was at the local jail. It was a single-floor set on the outskirts of Dalberton. The unimpressive building had thirty cells, more than half of which were always occupied. He knew Red was due to be released, and he was there to pick up his friend.

Red shielded his eyes from the bright sunlight as he exited the gate to freedom. When his eyes adjusted, he scanned the parking lot for any familiar faces waiting to usher him home.

There were two.

The first one he saw was Buster Cole; he was a very large man, heavily muscled and tattooed. This was Red's second-in-command, and he'd maintained control of the Riders while Red was in jail.

The other one was Al.

Seeing his childhood friend, Red quickly and quietly told Buster he would meet him back at the den. The lieutenant rode off, with his main lady following.

Red threw his hands up in frustration as he approached Al. "I can't even be out for ten minutes without you trying to save me!"

"It's good to see you too, Red." Al wasn't taking the bait.

"What do you want?"

"Get in. We'll talk on the way."

Red knew it wasn't worth arguing.

As they rumbled away, Red reminisced aloud. "I remember riding in Old Blue many times. She's still the only car I'd give up riding for."

Al smiled. "I know, and I respect that very much."

For a few miles the two old friends just enjoyed the sunshine, the rumble of the V8, and the open road. It was, for those few minutes, as if the trauma of the past and all of the hardships afterwards had never happened.

"Ok, Al, what's so important for you to come pick me up from jail?"

"I needed to tell you something in a place where you couldn't run away." With this statement, Al turned onto the freeway, knowing Red would be a captive audience, at least for a few minutes. "I prayed last night."

Red's face began to turn the same colour as his name. "No, Al, no."

"Just wait—you don't know what happened afterwards."

Red began to yell at this point. "*Al! I don't want—*"

"*I saw myself as a warrior of old!*" Al yelled, interrupting his passenger.

Red was stunned at this. "Wh-wh-what?" He looked ashen, as if he'd seen a ghost.

"After I finished praying, I went into the washroom. When I turned on the light, I saw myself as an ancient soldier!"

Red began to weep unexpectedly.

SEVEN
July 25, 1997

Red had just run back into his house and into his bedroom. Flopping face down on his bed, he let himself weep aloud, because everyone else was at Jeremy's. He was overwhelmed with the devastating death of his friend—and on the night he had trusted Jesus! Thinking about this last part made him cry out aloud.

"Lord Jesus, why would you let Jeremy die? Why?" He sobbed for a few minutes more then decided to wash his face off so that no one would know. He stepped into the bathroom and looked up to examine his face. The reflection in the mirror wasn't his but looked like a Roman-style soldier that was his size! Red couldn't understand what he was looking at, and the image moved as he moved.

He ran from the washroom and into the driveway, grabbing his bicycle and riding down the street, away from everyone. As he rode, his mind was frantically looking for explanations but not coming up with any.

He soon found himself riding slower and realized he was at the trail that went behind the "grouchy guy's" house. The guy in question was an old South Asian man, one of the first to move to Dalberton. He was well known for yelling at the people who took the path behind his yard. The city had assumed a portion of the back yards in this area and created a paved pathway. The owners had been financially compensated, but this man had never accepted the loss of his yard space.

Red stopped behind the grouch's back yard, staring at the house. The city had only put a chain link fence along the edges of the pathway. The old man looked out a window, and Red knew he was coming out, but he didn't move.

The back door opened and the man emerged, striding purposefully towards the youngster.

"Get off of my property! You don't have the right to be here!" Same as always, he still felt it was his land.

Red started to become overwhelmingly angry. He balled up his fists as the rage built.

"Did you hear me? *Get off of my land!*"

Without warning, Red lost control. Bending over, he picked up a large rock and hurled it at the man. The rock struck the man in the forehead, knocking him down and flooding his face with blood. Red suddenly realized what he'd done and rode back towards his home as fast as he could.

The demonic being couldn't have been happier.

EIGHT
Present Day

R ed let the tears flow a little while and then got himself under control.

"I can't believe it. I can't believe it. I'm not crazy," he said.

Al knew they had to pull over, so he turned off into the first rest area along the freeway. He shut the car off and looked at his lifelong friend.

"You've seen this!" he exclaimed in surprise.

"Yes."

"When? Where?" Al couldn't believe this. It was something he never expected.

"Right after Jeremy's funeral, at my house, right before I rode away."

"The day you hit the old guy with the rock?"

"Yeah. I went into the bathroom and saw my reflection as a tiny Roman soldier." He lay his head back on the headrest and sighed deeply.

"Why didn't you ever tell me?"

"I thought I was going crazy. Didn't you feel like that?"
Indeed he had.

"Yes, I did, but it's been almost twenty years for you."

"I know. I didn't think anyone would understand, and then there was all of the other trouble I got myself into." It was the first time that Red had admitted it.

"I'm glad you can see that now. I can explain the soldier thing if you want."

Red said he really wanted to understand it.

Al spent the next half hour explaining the spiritual side of life to him. At the end of it, Red wore a look on his face that Al recognized. Looking directly at him, he asked a serious question.

"Do you think it's time to pray again?"

Red nodded, as he knew this was it for him.

Al listened as Red poured his heart out to the Lord and confessed his sins openly. After he said "Amen," he looked up, and Al realized that he was viewing him spiritually. He shifted into the spiritual view as well and took a look at his friend. He saw another armour-clad soldier sitting in the car with him. As Al examined his friend, he saw only light emanating from him, and he knew Red had been healed by the Lord. The other thing they saw was that Red's cloak was yellow in colour; neither of them knew what that meant.

But they knew who to talk to about it.

NINE
July 25, 1997

Sergeant Whitaker had arrived at the Harnett home a couple of hours after Red threw the rock. He had a serious look on his face, and after talking to Red's parents, he looked at the young boy.

"You know why I'm here, Red. This is very serious." The youth nodded. "The first thing you need to know is that the old man isn't dead."

Red looked up at this. "He isn't? But his face was so covered in blood."

"Yes, that's because heads bleed a lot. He's going to be fine—just a few stitches."

Red exhaled heavily, obviously relieved.

"There's still a punishment involved, and unfortunately, I'm not the one to decide what that will be." Red looked at his parents. "No, they aren't either." Red looked confused. "You're going to have to go to Juvenile Court." The boy's eyes grew wide. "It won't take place for about a month or so, but you *must* attend. Do you understand?" He gave Red a stern look.

Red nodded, looking terrified. The experienced officer knew he got it.

"Now, I want you to tell me why you threw the rock."

Red struggled for a moment and then admitted his anger about Jeremy. He also described how the old man had harassed the three boys many times when they'd ride down the path. He did *not*, however, tell the cop about what he'd seen in the mirror. He knew that would get him sent to a "shrink," and he didn't want that.

"Ok, I understand. We've had complaints about him from others. I also understand that you just came from your friend's funeral. I'll make note of those facts in my report; it will probably help you in court."

"Really? So I won't go to juvie?"

The sergeant's mouth was grim but his eyes smiled. "No. This is the first time you've done something serious. They'll most likely give you a few months of community service."

Red knew what that was. He'd seen people wearing orange shirts cleaning up garbage in Dalberton. That was the most common community service, and he figured he could do that if he had to.

"Oh, ok, I guess that's not so bad." He felt relieved, because he knew he deserved far worse.

"I need to talk to your mom and dad now. Don't forget about court."

"I won't."

He never forgot that day.

Present Day

Al had called Ben and arranged to meet with him at Murphy's. They were driving back into town when Red made a request.

"Drop me at the Den. I want to pick up Scarlett." His old friend gave him a suspicious look. "Don't worry, they need to see me there as well. I'll be at Murphy's." He gave a thumbs up signal. "Thumb swear." Al relaxed at this and dropped his friend off at the Den.

The thumb swear was something they'd done for decades. It started when they were five years old, that first year in school when they were still establishing their friendship. It was a promise, unbreakable and unchangeable, between the two of them. Neither of them had ever broken it, nor would they.

Al dropped Red off and headed towards the truck stop, with an admonishment to the biker of "Don't be long."

Red had told him to shut up and walked into the communal home of the biker group. He was met with several and various forms of "Hey" or "Yo," along with a few cheers. He walked through the large common room towards the garage, passing many bikers and their ladies in various forms of relaxation. Buster approached him from the garage area with his lady in tow.

"That pig give you any trouble? You've been gone longer than I expected." There was suspicion in his question as well as genuine concern.

"No, nothing to worry about; he's just a childhood friend concerned about my recent descent. Nothing more."

Buster laughed at this. "Descent into hell, right?"

Red needed to be careful how he responded. "I need to go for a ride. It's been too long. Is she ready?"

"Yeah. You want some company?"

"No, I need some solo time with Scarlett."

Red's lieutenant nodded. "Ok, Boss." He said this word with just a hint of derision. "Whatever you say."

Red knew he needed to flex a little muscle, so he got in Buster's face. "Don't forget it," he growled at the number two man, who, instead of getting angry, seemed to greatly enjoy the exchange.

As the leader wheeled the chopper onto the street and rumbled away, he mumbled under his breath. "Someday it'll be you who has to remember it."

ELEVEN

August 29, 1997

The court date was set for a Friday. Red and his parents were early to the courthouse, so they sat on a bench in the hallway outside of Courtroom 3. A myriad of troubled youth came and went, some looking scared; others, angry. A few of these young people were outspokenly defiant about being there. One of them came in handcuffed between two guards and looking fiercely unhappy. He was spouting off colourful obscenities about the justice system and his hatred of it.

As he was passing Red and his parents, he suddenly bent towards him, putting his face right up to the youth's. "Don't trust them! They lie!" he shouted to the younger boy. This got him a hard pull back from Red and an even harder wallop on the back of his head.

"Behave yourself!" the guard ordered.

Any other delinquent would have realized that he was out of line and submitted to the order. Not this boy. Growling in hatred, he struck the guard on his left with his elbow, hard. The guard reeled from the blow, staggering away from his attacker. The youth then brought both of his hands up, clasped together into one fist, and struck the other guard under the chin. The second guard's head was knocked back, and he slumped to the floor unconscious.

More guards came running to subdue the attacker. After several blows, ending with a knee in his back and his face on the floor, he was overcome. As they led him to his courtroom, he continued to scream profanities for anyone to hear.

"The system is corrupt! They beat children! You'll never be free!"

Red was never so scared in all of his life.

TWELVE

Present Day

Al was having a smoke while leaning up against Old Blue when Ben pulled up next to him. Ben had Kranti with him, and he put his tailgate down and invited the men to sit on it.

The three exchanged greetings, and Al handed Ben a coffee that he had ready. He apologized to Kranti, not knowing he'd be there. Kranti wasn't offended and said he'd wait to get one. Al then filled in the other men on what had happened with Red earlier that day.

"Are you serious? The leader of the notorious biker gang has turned to Jesus? Praise God!" Ben exclaimed joyously.

"Incredible what the Lord can do." Kranti laughed.

"I know, right? It's an awesome thing, but I'm so very happy that my friend is fully free. Praise God, indeed," Al stated.

Just as he was saying this, the familiar sound of a V-twin engine was heard. Scarlett rolled into the lot, carrying Red.

The biker leader walked up to the trio and they exchanged greetings. He then asked them to wait while he went in for a coffee.

"I'll come with you. I need one, too," Kranti said.

As the duo entered the truck stop, they were both a little uneasy because of the hospital event. They also knew that a conversation had to happen between them about it. Red spoke first.

"I'm sorry for … the hospital," he offered, referring to the time he'd held Kranti and his family hostage and had threatened to kill them.

Normally Kranti would be angry, but he had been changing since he became a believer in Jesus.

"I understand. I was a very angry and confused man before I met Jesus."

"Why were you angry?"

"I never wanted to come to this country. That was my wife's idea. I also had a lot of prejudice against how Western people live."

They got their coffees and would have continued their conversation, but they were interrupted by an exasperated comment.

"Oh, you've got to be kidding me!"

Sammy.

The young blond-haired man stood in angry astonishment in front of the two men. He was obviously very unhappy to see them talking together like old friends.

"Sammy, we need to talk," Red told the younger man.

"Now you want to talk? I almost shot him because of you, and then you threw me away!" He pointed at Kranti as he said this, his face red with rage.

"I was wrong … about so much. Please come outside and talk."

"I'm not interested in talking with you anymore."

With this statement, Sammy stormed out of the door and strode away from the other men. Moments later, he rode past the four men, who were again talking at Ben's pickup. It was clear that he saw all of them. Witnessing this, Red worried aloud. "Somehow I don't think this is a good thing."

THIRTEEN

September 27, 1997

R ed had been ordered to do community service for a month, cleaning up the sidewalks and walking paths of Dalberton. He was given a light sentence, partially because it was his first offence and partially because of Sergeant Whitaker's report. He was on his last day of his sentence, and he was happy he was so close to being finished.

"I guess this is your last day, huh?" his cleanup partner for the day, Logan Lincoln, asked.

"Yeah, I'm so glad it's almost over," Red admitted.

"What are you going to do with your time now?"

"I'm not sure. I'd like to ride my bike some more, since I'll have time and winter is coming."

"What kind of bike do you have? I love motorcycles." The older boy had misunderstood.

"Oh, I meant my BMX, not a motorcycle. I'm not old enough to ride one of those."

Logan got a strange look on his face. "I started riding dirt bikes when I was eight." He then leaned closer. "My dad has a few that need a lot of work, but maybe you could get one of those."

Red was excited at the idea, but he didn't have money for that. "I don't have any money, and I'd have to talk to my parents about it. I don't think they'd let me."

Logan had seen the light in the younger boy's eyes at the idea of having a motorcycle. "Let me talk to my dad. He might make a good deal for a friend of mine. Just give me your phone number and I'll have my dad talk to yours."

Red was a bit unsure, but Logan had been nice to him, so he decided to trust him.

They exchanged phone numbers and continued with their work until the day ended a short time later. Red and the other boys were loaded onto the "juvie van" and taken back to the detention centre, where they handed in their equipment and vests. Red signed his papers at the signing station and was given his stamped copies saying he'd served his sentence.

On the drive home, Red told his dad, Rick, about Logan's offer. Rick was a bit cautious but agreed to talk with Larry, Logan's father. Red was so excited when he arrived home that he rode his bike over to Al's home and told him about it.

"You're getting a motorcycle? That's so cool! I'm getting something, too; come and see." It was very clear that Al was just as excited as Red. They entered the Mitchells' garage, but the only thing Red saw was the old muscle-car that belonged to Al's dad, parked where it had been for decades.

"What am I supposed to see here?" he asked aloud.

"Old Blue. She's gonna be mine when I turn sixteen. Dad said we can work on her until then to get her ready."

"Really? Wow! That's amazing, Al. I always loved Old Blue."

It was true. Red had ridden in Old Blue several times over the years, until it had been parked a few years ago. He always loved going for rides with his friend in the classic machine. The two boys congratulated each other and enjoyed an evening together for the first time since Jeremy's death.

Neither of them knew how much these vehicles would affect their futures.

FOURTEEN

Present Day

The four men had been talking about spiritual matters and enjoying coffee and donuts for about thirty minutes. Ben and Kranti had been explaining the spiritual view that was accessible to them and how to switch back and forth. Al and Red were learning a lot from the more experienced Christians, and a good time was being had by all.

Suddenly, Nathaniel and Ramiel—Ben's and Kranti's guardians respectively—landed forcefully with two other angels. The lead angel turned to Ben.

"Trouble is coming. Prepare yourselves," he admonished.

"What is it, Nathaniel?" Ben questioned, knowing it was serious.

"Look."

All of the angels turned and pointed to a large group of bikers. Buster, rolling along at the head of the group, was leading a group of about thirty men. His black bike, sporting painted skulls on the tank, presented an imposing sight with the huge man sitting on it.

The greater threat, however, was the very large group of demons with the riders. There were various evil beings, some large and some small, but all looking ready for a fight.

The bikers surrounded the four men and stepped off the motorcycles. Buster approached Red with mockery in his eyes, judging the situation.

"So you hang out with cops and Christians now? Is this the direction you're planning on taking the club?" It was very accusatory.

"Since when do I answer to you, Buster? I'm the leader of the Riders." Red was angry at being questioned, but one of the angels held a hand up to him, warning him to back off. He assumed this was his guardian, but this wasn't the time for introductions.

Red stepped back as instructed and, without warning, a massive demon appeared where he'd just been. It materialized out of a black mist, all of which swirled and seemed to cling together until it formed the evil being. The being was larger than any of them could have imagined—except Ben. He'd faced off with this enemy before.

Satan.

The evil leader turned towards the eager group of demons and the bikers with them. He held up a hand towards the large group.

"Wait." It was only one word, but it seemed to freeze the bikers in place. The other demons knew better than to question the command. They paused as instructed and awaited the order of their superior. Turning back to the Christians, he spoke in a gravelly, deep, and menacing voice.

"You men are troublesome, and I'm getting tired of all of you."

"Get used to it." Al spoke directly to the enemy before them.

"Ah, the Protector. Haven't you and your 'enlightened' friend learned not to mess with me?"

"What are you talking about?" Red asked.

"Jeremy."

One word, one name, but it meant everything to them.

"You killed him?" Both spoke it as one.

Deep chuckling emanated from the demon leader. "I have done so much more than that, and I will do even more if you don't back off. I have plans for Dalberton, and they don't include you four."

"We don't take orders from you. The Lord Jesus is our king, and we will obey him, not you," Ben shot back.

"Benjamin," the leader growled, "you must think that somehow you actually hurt me in our last meeting, but"—he held up the hand Ben had driven his spiritual sword through—"as you can see, I am unharmed. I told you that you can't defeat me."

"Jesus has already defeated you. I don't have to. I just have to help others find the Saviour." Ben was defiant in his stance.

"I should tell you, Jeremy wasn't the only one I killed."

A suggestive silence followed.

"Nancy?" Ben faltered at the sudden epiphany, and his rival laughed loudly.

"Resist the devil and he will flee from you!" Kranti had listened to enough from the father of lies, and he began to shine brightly.

The fight was on.

FiFTEEN

July 11, 1998

L ogan had been helping Red and his dad with the chopper build. He'd been visiting many weekends and had even brought a few needed parts. He said they were gifts from his dad, whom Red had met and liked very much. Larry had even allowed Red to visit the Den— that's what he called the home where most of the motorcycle club members lived. The teen boys had spent many hours there looking at motorcycles and parts.

During their time at the Den, Red had learned much about motorcycles, such as how to disassemble an engine and rebuild it, as well as the other mechanical parts. Larry had even begun to show him how to use a paint gun and how to properly mix the paint to make it ready to spray onto the parts. This had been an exhilarating time for Red, and he'd already imagined how he wanted his bike to look and sound when it was complete.

There were two places within the Den that the boys were strictly forbidden to enter. The trailers at the very back of the lot were the homes of the members, and the boys were told to stay away from there. The bar and lounge area within the main building were also off limits, for obvious reasons. Being boys, they did sneak a quick peek into the bar now and then, just out of curiosity.

An evil being watched all of this from the spiritual side and was pleased.

• • •

In the downtown area, another hit and run killing was being investigated by Sergeant Whitaker. This time it was a married couple who'd been shopping with their two-year-old son. The parents were both dead, but somehow the boy was miraculously unharmed. The sergeant was taking statements at this point and feeling a tug of memory playing in his mind.

"I couldn't believe it—he just drove straight at them!" A distraught witness was recounting the event. "He didn't even slow down afterwards. He just kept on going like he didn't care."

Like he didn't care. Why is that so familiar? "Did you get a good look at the driver?"

"No. It was weird—the car was so dark inside that I couldn't see him."

Weird. The car was dark inside. Why do these statements ring a bell? "Ok, what about the car itself? Did you see the plate?"

"It was a very large, all-black, older car. I only saw the last three digits of the plate—4N5."

Suddenly, it hit the police sergeant with full force.

A large black car.

Jeremy Parker.

Sixteen

Present Day

The battle commenced with Kranti's outspoken resistance to Satan's mockery. He let his light shine brightly, instantly dissolving the smallest and even some of the medium-sized demons. His attack caused the angels to move into position and begin their own assault of this evil army. One of them moved close to Red and began to instruct him.

"Use your gift to see what the enemy's movements will be."

"How do I do that?" Red wasn't even aware that he had an ability.

"Focus on the spirit inside you—feel his presence."

Red focused inwardly and sensed a warm, comforting spirit within himself. Concentrating on this new sensation, he began to get a sense of precognition. He could see what the enemy would do a few seconds beforehand, so he relayed this to the others.

"Ben, on your left!" A sneak attack averted.

While he was doing his part, Al's guardian gave him instruction on his own ability.

"You have the ability to project a shield; use it when Red lets you know."

Al focused on what he now knew to be the Holy Spirit's leading. He was late for the first shot that came his way, taking a hit to his sword arm. Learning from that mistake, he was ready when Red called out to him.

"Al, use your shield!"

Success! A volley of fiery darts was blocked by a gigantic transparent shield. The battle continued on, both spiritually and physically. The demonic forces fought spiritually while the bikers, unaware of the spiritual battle, threw punches and kicks at the Christians. It was hard for them to fight on both fronts, and the battle was becoming wearying for the four men.

Suddenly, sirens could be heard in the distance, and they knew that police forces would be there in minutes. Red saw his opportunity for victory over his challenger and took it. Driving his fist into Buster's jaw, he knocked his opponent out, causing the rest of the bikers to stop their physical attack.

Ben also saw the spiritual opportunity and nodded at Kranti. They both struck at Satan with their swords while quoting, "Resist the devil and he will flee from you!!"

Satan, hit by both swords and hearing those words, did just that. He fled, vanishing in a cloud of black smoke, and his troops did likewise.

Several police cars raced into the lot and surrounded the group of fighters. They quickly subdued the scene and began asking questions. After they understood what had happened, they put the bikers in handcuffs. When they started putting cuffs on Red, Al stepped in to defend his friend.

"Wait, he's with us."

The officer looked surprised. "Are you sure, Al? He's the leader of the group."

"He didn't lead this group—that was Buster."

As the police led him away, Buster, recovered from the punch he'd taken, spat various profanities and threats towards the four Christian men.

It was obvious that this wasn't the end of it.

SEVENTEEN

July 18, 1998

Sergeant Whitaker was looking into unsolved murders involving hit and runs. The light had gone on in his mind after the witness statements from the latest killing downtown. He needed to see if there'd been similar vehicular deaths. He'd found two more in the six days he'd been looking, and that alone made him more committed to finding this murderer.

It was a slow process because the filing was still mostly on paper. The Dalberton police force had only just begun to file reports digitally. It was also slow going because he had to fit the researching into the rest of his workday. He had an inkling, though, that he'd find many more of these events, and he needed a solid case to present to his captain.

• • •

It had been a year to the day since Jeremy had died. Devin Jackson was at Al's house talking with both of the boys. He was the youth pastor from Harmony Fellowship Church, and he wanted to see how the boys were doing.

They were in the garage working on Old Blue, trying to fix the brakes, when the pastor arrived.

"Hello, boys."

"Hey," they replied in unison.

"I know you guys are probably trying not to think about Jeremy today."

"That's why we're working on my car," Al honestly answered.

"Seems like a good distraction." He smiled.

"It was working until you showed up." Red wasn't happy to see the pastor.

"I'm sorry, I didn't mean to stir up bad feelings, I just wanted to see how you guys are doing." An awkward silence followed, so the man tried a different tactic. "I was hoping to see you boys at the church again."

"I'm gonna get a pop," Red stated and went into the house.

"We can't come back—not after that night," Al told the pastor.

The darkness was blissfully happy.

EIGHTEEN

Present Day

I t was the first Sunday after their return to the Lord and the first time either of them had been back to Harmony. The friends were nervous and excited. It was a strange feeling to have as an adult, but there it was. As they prepared to walk in, the two friends looked at each other, both of them thinking about Jeremy. A familiar voice called out to them warmly.

"Red! Al! Oh, praise God! I've been praying for this day!"

Devin Jackson.

They both grinned widely and greeted the youth pastor with a warm handshake.

"Hi, Devin," Red replied. "Sorry about the last time we spoke."

"To see you here today makes that day worth it."

Red was almost brought to tears by that. All he could muster before clearing his throat was "Thank you."

"I hope you don't mind, but I invited my club to join me here today." Red gestured towards the group of bikers that had pulled into the church parking lot.

"Of course! They are all welcome. We want them to find Jesus, too."

Red waved the group over and led them into the church to find seats.

The sermon that day was from Luke 15:11–32, the parable of the prodigal son, and it seemed very appropriate to Al and Red. The pastor spoke on how the father in the parable didn't care what his son had done. He loved him and was overjoyed that his son had finally come home to him. It was a reminder to Al and Red that Jesus had been waiting with open arms for them to return to Him. They both felt such peace and joy—the exact feeling they'd had the night Jeremy died. They both silently wept in love for Jesus.

Dark forces had been watching, and they left to seek their leader.

NINETEEN

January 8, 2001

D etective Whitaker was elated to have earned the promotion from sergeant to this new position. He now had more freedom to investigate cases he felt were important, which allowed him to seriously dig into his suspicions about a vehicular serial killer in Dalberton. He had discovered three more incidents recently, but the process was still slow.

He walked into Captain Dahlstrom's office to announce his return to work in his new role. Sitting in a chair across the desk from his superior, he waited for him to finish what sounded like an important phone call. After another minute, the captain hung up the phone and gave him a serious look.

"Well, Detective Whitaker, I guess you've convinced the chief of the need to investigate this vehicular killer." A grim smile accompanied the announcement. "Just be careful with this one. Remember that you're working alone due to lack of partner availability."

Whitaker nodded. "Yes, sir."

"You're going to need proof, so find it."

Another nod and "Yes, sir" from the new detective and he was dismissed.

He was determined and hopeful, so he began to rifle through files.

In the spiritual realm, a low growl could be heard.

TWENTY

Present Day

For God sent not his Son into the world
to condemn the world; but that the world
through him might be saved. (John 3:17)

t was a verse that reached many of the bikers that Sunday morning. Many of the men wanted to know more
about what this meant, so they went off in a group
with Ben, Al, Red, Dave, and a few more of the men of the
church into a private room to talk and pray.

The biker ladies also wanted to learn about Jesus, so
Doreen, Kathy, and some ladies from Harmony talked
with them separate from the men.

Many souls were won for Christ that day and great
joy was felt. The new believers were stunned at the change
they found in themselves. The experienced Christians
helped explain the new side of life these new believers had
found. It was a long day of explaining and training, but it
was well spent and enjoyed by all.

Warriors of a wide variety were born that day. Prayer, Support, a Protector, a couple of Evangelists, and even a Healer, just to name a few. Bibles were passed out to all and scripture passages suggested for study. The new Christians were told about Bible study groups and times, and they all confirmed that they would attend.

A few of the bikers and their ladies thought the others were nuts, so they left of their own accord to return to the Den.

TWENTY-ONE

March 16, 2002

A l had just gone on a ride-along with Detective Whitaker and he loved it. He had chosen this as a possible career path because of the genuine care and concern he'd felt from Detective Whitaker at the time of Jeremy's death. The ride-along was a part of Dalberton High School's Career Information and Planning week. It was a huge event, allowing students to explore various jobs in their final year of school.

Now seventeen, Al knew he needed to find something to do with his life, and bringing justice sounded very appealing to him. He wanted to bring peace and safety to his community, especially since Jeremy's killer had never been found.

"So what did you think of seeing some of what I do every day?"

"I love it!" Al replied enthusiastically.

The detective chuckled and nodded knowingly.

"Did you get your information packet?"

"Yep, got it right here." He held up the pamphlet full of police training information and an application form for the Dalberton Police College.

They arrived at Al's home, and the teen thanked the detective again. Seeing Red in his garage, he went in the side door.

Red was putting the finishing touches on some hand-painted pinstripes on Scarlett. The bike had been totally transformed. Over the past five years, it had gone from a rusty frame and engine to a fully built, beautifully painted chopper. It gleamed brightly with chrome bars, pipes, forks, and spoked wheels. It was also painted a myriad of reds, including crimson and scarlet, of course. The metal-flake ratio changed according to the shade of red used, and it was spectacular.

"Wow! Man, you've really built her perfectly. If I were a biker, this is the only one I'd want to ride!" He was grinning from ear to ear.

"Thanks, Al. If you ever want to trade for Old Blue, I'll do it."

"Haha, good luck with that."

Red finished the last brush stroke and stood back to examine his work. "Not bad."

"Not bad? More like perfect," his friend rebuked him.

"Thanks. I guess it's better than I realize. What do you have there?" He had just noticed the packet Al was carrying.

The moment had come, and Al was worried because he knew what Red thought about cops. Taking a breath to calm himself, he revealed the contents of the packet.

"It's the career information package to join the Dalberton Police Force."

"Really? You're going forward with that?" Red's voice was tinged with disdain.

"I've tried to tell you that I feel that by becoming a cop, I can help keep others from being killed." He was getting a little angry with his friend.

"And I've told you that they haven't done anything to find Jeremy's killer. Nothing at all." Now Red was angry.

"You're wrong. Detective Whitaker has been looking into it."

"Detective now, is it?" Red spat the words. "Just what has he done?"

"He said he can't share that with me—it's a cop thing. They have to protect their findings. It's for when they go to court."

Red held his hand up. "I don't want to hear anymore about it. You go be a cop. I've already become a member of the Lunatics anyways; they'll take care of me."

"I will be a cop and I'll make a difference. I'll show you." With that, Al stepped out the door. Turning back, he gave his friend one last bit of advice. "Be careful, Red. I've heard bad things about the Lunatics."

The dark being from the night Jeremy died was laughing hard.

TWENTY-TWO

Present Day

R ed had returned to the Den to announce the conversion of the bikers who had chosen to follow Jesus. He then extended an invitation to any of the others who wanted to know about Christianity. After this, he made another announcement that he knew would have a huge impact and probably be met with serious resistance.

"So now that you know what's happened to the majority of our club, we're going to make some changes." All heads turned abruptly in his direction. If he didn't have their attention before, he surely did now. "We'll no longer be known as 'Red's Riders.' I am officially changing the club name to 'Redeemed Riders.'"

Some comments of disagreement could be heard, as could some supportive ones. Red held up his hand to the questions.

"This is because enough members have become Christians that I feel the Lord leading me to dedicate this group to Him."

A few colourful comments were made at this, quite loudly from some, and Red continued. "Those who don't want to be part of a Christian organization aren't required to stay with us. You are free to leave if you choose to."

Some men confirmed that they'd be leaving, again quite loudly and offensively.

"We're going to start cleaning this place up as well. The bar is going to be converted into a communal study and prayer room."

More loud resistance. Some of the long-time members walked out, spewing vocally their displeasure with the decision.

"That's all for now. Those who want to stay are welcome." With that, Red scanned the room spiritually and saw many demons angrily looking in his direction. They followed the unhappy humans out the door as they left.

Red knew it wasn't going to be so easy as making an announcement, but he was committed to making this change for his Lord and Saviour.

What he wasn't aware of was the group gathering at a private location and who was leading them.

Buster.

TWENTY-THREE

January 9, 2006

Whitaker had been called to Captain Dahlstrom's office, and he was pretty sure what it was about. His investigation into the car killer in Dalberton had netted him nothing. He'd spent five years and countless hours trying to identify this killer but to no avail.

"You know what this is about." A statement not a question.

The detective nodded.

"Yeah, it's been five years. I know."

"The chief just told me to put it on hold for now. We'll keep it open in case we get anything new on it." He could see the disappointment on the detective's face. "I'm sorry, Dan. I know this one is important to you." He knew the story of what had happened so many years ago to young Jeremy, and he understood the detective's feelings. Whitaker thanked the captain, knowing he meant it, and left the office.

Satan was happy.

• • •

Jason Satanovic was communicating with the spiritual being he worshipped.

It wasn't Jesus.

"Master, what instruction do you have for me?" He bowed in complete submission to this dark entity.

"The police have halted their search for you. Be still for now. I will return when it's time for further action," Satan instructed the man.

Jason had been worshipping Satan for many years and had followed his every demand. He was the driver of the black car, the murderer who'd been killing in Dalberton for over thirty years. It was only through Satan's instructions that he'd evaded capture, and he knew it.

"Of course, I obey as always." With that submission, Satan vanished.

TWENTY-FOUR

Present Day

Two days later, Buster Cole was addressing the furious group of bikers that had assembled. He knew it was time to make a strong move to take over the club and put a stop to those Christians once and for all.

"You're all here because you aren't happy with our leader, as you know I'm not," he growled. "So now it's time to end this farce and take back our home. I should have been the leader, not Red. Larry made a mistake when he chose him instead of me."

Other members voiced their assent with comments like "yeah" and "for sure." Many commented about the Christian influence being unwanted as well. Buster was greatly encouraged by these comments and continued with his plan to shut down Red and the Christians.

Sammy Silverton was watching and listening, but he had a bad feeling about this gathering. The next thing Buster said confirmed his fears.

"I've gathered some weapons for us. I'm done with playing around with fist-fights. It's time to get serious about that church and Red. Do you agree?" It wasn't so much a request as it was a confirmation of being committed to Buster's leadership. The bikers knew what this meant if they chose to follow him, but they were out of their home and felt that they didn't have a choice. These were some tough men, and women as well, used to a life of serious violence, so shooting people didn't bother these bikers at all.

The individual bikers each chose a weapon and waited expectantly for directions on where and when they would attack their enemies. They were eager to get back their home and the lifestyle they'd lost.

Sammy walked forward and chose a weapon as well, because he knew if he didn't, he'd be questioned about it. He had no desire to kill anyone, and he was waiting for the right time to tell Buster that he wanted out of this.

"I've learned that they have a Bible study and prayer night tonight at that church. We're going to give them something to pray about. They'll be finishing and coming outside in ten minutes, which gives us just enough time to saddle up and get there. Let's go."

TWENTY-FIVE

November 18, 2006

Buster Cole was furious. Larry Lincoln, the leader of the Lunatics, had just announced that he was stepping down as leader. He and his son were leaving, and his successor would be Red Harnett.

They were still all gathered together in the common room watching as the unique leadership tattoo was applied to Red's right forearm. It was a crazy looking face with an open mouth. The year leadership was appointed was tattooed across the loose-hanging tongue. Anyone found with the tattoo who wasn't a present or past leader was held down and a branding iron used to obliterate the false claim. They took it that seriously.

When the tattoo was finished, Red stood up from the chair and raised his right arm to show the fresh badge. Cheers resounded in support of the new boss, and then the drinking began in celebration of the next generation. Buster watched as Larry gave some whispered instruction to Red and then followed when he and his son left on their bikes.

The two Lincolns rode to a dirty alley in the industrial section of the city. Buster had discreetly followed them, parking out of sight and walking into the alley behind them. They were obviously waiting for someone to meet them, and he heard them talking to each other.

"I didn't realize we had fifteen more minutes before the meeting. Sorry, son."

"No problem, Dad, we can wait. It's no big deal." The younger man looked at his father. "Thanks for making Red the next boss; he's gonna be great."

"I think so too, and you're welcome. I know you and Red have become close friends. That's why we're doing this. He needs to be protected from Buster."

Logan nodded in agreement. "Detective Whitaker needs to know what Buster has done."

Buster stepped out of the shadows, pistol raised, and addressed the two bikers.

"What exactly does he need to know?"

Surprised, the Lincolns turned around to face the unexpected arrival of their foe. Seeing the weapon, Larry put a hand up, pleading with the gunman.

"Please, Buster, don't hurt my son. He's just a kid."

"So is the guy you appointed as the next boss."

"Buster, I know what you did, the direction you'd take the club in. I'm ok with drugs, extortion, and fist-fights, but not murder."

"Too bad." Buster stated flatly, then he fired three shots, fatally injuring the elder Lincoln man.

Logan jumped off his bike as his father fell to the ground. "Dad!" He desperately tried to stop the blood that poured from the wounds.

"Sorry, kid," Buster stated. When the young man turned to face him, he shot him to death as well. With that, he returned to his bike and rode a different way back to the Den.

There was a darkness deeper than the night travelling with Buster.

Twenty-six

Present Day

S ammy had waited until the other bikers left and then quickly turned off on a different route. He desperately needed to beat the others to the church so he could warn them. Racing at speeds well above the limit, he knew he was risking attracting a cop, but that might be good right now. As he pulled into the church parking lot, he saw a few of the members just coming out the doors. He rode directly up to them. They looked up in alarm as he began yelling.

"Stop! Go back inside!" He leapt off the orange chopper.

"What is it?" Red had come out to see what was going on.

"Buster is coming with a group. They have guns!" The sound of many V-twins could be heard not far off. Red ushered the others back into the foyer, along with Sammy. Just as he closed the doors, the large group of bikers rode into the lot and began to fire upon the church.

Bullets could be heard impacting the walls and doors as the people inside got further into the building. They crouched behind the heaviest items—pews and desks—to keep out of the line of fire. Some of them began to pray aloud, and after a few seconds, they were praying in unison.

"Lord Jesus, protect us from this attack, we pray. Protect your building, we pray. Show these people the error of their way." They continued on as the bullets seemed to be endless, and some even managed to penetrate the building, whizzing past them furiously.

The outside air suddenly became much quieter. The only sound was the many motorcycle engines, idling at first then quickly accelerating away. Another sound became clearer and closer. Sirens. The police cars pulled up front as Al and Red were opening the doors to check on things.

One of the other ladies from the Bible study called out suddenly.

"Come quick! He's been hit!"

The police came running along with the two friends.

It was Sammy, lying on his back. He'd been hit several times, and it was serious.

One officer called for an ambulance while others were securing the scene and checking for any other injuries.

Red requested to accompany Sammy to the hospital, and they allowed it.

TWENTY-SEVEN

December 7, 2007

Detective Whitaker was worn out. He'd been working multiple cases. Some he had found answers for, some he had solved, and some he'd come up completely empty. It had been mentally and emotionally draining on him, and he couldn't wait for Christmas vacation time at the end of the month.

At this moment, though, he had a little time to look into the serial killer again. The captain had been understanding towards this matter as long as he only put small amounts of time into it. The chief hadn't lifted his restriction on the case as of yet. He knew he'd missed something. He was looking at his notes on the Silvertons and Jeremy when it stood out to him.

The license plate!

He knew he'd written down notes about the plate number in both cases.

The first three digits: 547. The young Al Mitchell had provided this part.

The last three were 4N5, the witness from the Silvertons' killing said.

He wrote them together and looked at something that didn't make any sense to him.

547 4N5

That wasn't a normal plate number—not for a Dalberton vehicle. He didn't understand what it meant, and he was too tired to dig further right now. He was packing up his things for the night when Sergeant Al Mitchell walked out of the locker room. From his street clothes, Whitaker knew he must be done for the night.

"Hey, how's our newest sergeant?"

Al grinned at this. "I'm pretty good, but starving. You eat lately?"

"Actually, I think I forgot. You know how it is."

"I do. Let's go catch up at Murphy's. I'll buy."

He wasn't going to turn that down.

"Alright, let me finish up here and I'll meet you in the parking lot."

True to his word, he met Al next to his car in just a few minutes.

"Hey, you mind giving me a ride home after? I don't drive Old Blue in winter. Took a taxi in today."

"Oh sure, buy me supper in exchange for a ride." The old detective was laughing and so was the new sergeant.

They set off towards Murphy's, looking forward to the meal, when Whitaker mentioned the odd license plate.

"Hey"—he pulled out his notepad, handing it to the younger man—"do you make anything of this? I can't understand it."

Al took a look and recognized it right away, paling a bit at the sight of it.

"Is this the complete license plate?"

Whitaker nodded.

"I just don't understand it. It's not a normal plate for here, or anywhere else that I know of." Al was looking at the numbers, and one letter in particular, when his face lit up. "It's leetspeak."

The older man, by the look on his face, had no idea.

"I learned about this while I was in training. It's a newer form of communicating, mostly used on the net."

A furrowed brow was the response. "What's it mean?"

"If I'm translating this correctly … SATANS."

It was Detective Whitaker's turn to go pale.

TWENTY-EIGHT

Present Day

S ammy had been rushed into surgery, and Red had no idea how he was doing. He was pacing the waiting room when Al and the others from Harmony arrived.

"What do you know?" Al asked.

"Nothing. They took him into surgery right away and I've just been here waiting."

"Ok, let's all sit down and pray for him." This was Devin, of course.

"Right," Red said. "I forgot. Sorry."

"That's ok; it seems like this young man is important to you."

"I'm kind of responsible for this, I think. I'll explain after we pray."

"Maybe you should lead us in prayer then."

Red was eager to do so. "Lord Jesus," he started, "please don't let Sammy die. I feel so responsible for him being in this situation, I'm sorry for my part in it. In the name of Jesus. Amen." Short but heartfelt and to the point.

They then took turns praying for the young man who had gotten shot warning them. As they prayed, they felt a comforting presence spread among them until they had peace about Sammy.

Lifting his eyes after the final prayer had ended, Red saw a heavenly assistant beside each of them. He'd learned of the angelic defenders assigned to each Christian, but it was an amazing sight nonetheless. He felt a strange hand on his shoulder and looked at the angel beside him.

"This wasn't your fault. He chose his path, but don't worry—he will live."

The others gathered there were still in the spiritual view and had heard this as well. They began to sing praises to the Lord; it wasn't loud, but others in the waiting area could hear them. One nurse in particular gave them a stern look and admonished them to keep quiet. They just kept on singing.

"How are you all so happy that this young man got shot? He might still die! Don't you care? You Christians are so unfeeling!" With that final accusation, she stormed off. Devin felt the need to share some scripture with the group.

"In Matthew 5:44, Jesus says, '*But I say unto you, love your enemies, bless them that curse you, do good to them that hate you, and pray for them which despitefully use you, and persecute you.'* This is what God's Word says about these things, so let's pray for this young nurse as well, that she might find Jesus herself through this."

So they did just that.

TWENTY-NINE

December 7, 2007

S atan suddenly materialized in front of his servant, surprising the human. Jason bowed quickly in submission to his master. This pleased Satan every time. It didn't remove the anger he felt at the moment, however.

"The police detective is getting too close to discovering you. I want you to stop him. Take an unknown vehicle, something not registered to you, and kill him," the evil being commanded. "Afterwards, crush the vehicle and destroy any evidence that you were there."

"Yes, I will make this happen. As always, I obey."

• • •

Al and the detective had enjoyed a good meal at the truck-stop and were now heading to his home. The diner had been packed and they were unable to comfortably talk about the case while they ate. So they had waited until they were back in the car to continue with the discussion about the license plate.

They agreed that they needed to do an online search of the licensing database. Given their current tired state, they also agreed that it could wait until morning.

A light snow had begun to fall while they were eating, and it had built up to a couple of inches on the road. Whitaker was a very experienced driver, though, so he maintained control without a problem.

They were rounding a left-hand curve on a small cliff-side rise. The detective was taking care because this was an especially slippery spot. Before they finished the curve, bright lights behind them suddenly bathed their car in blinding light. A solid hit to the rear of the car sent it sliding over the cliff's edge!

THIRTY

Present Day

S ammy was out of surgery and resting in a private room while Red sat by his side. The doctors had said that it was a successful surgery and it was a miracle that the bullets had so narrowly missed anything vital. Red knew it was indeed a miracle—provided by the Lord Himself, he was sure.

It had been a long night, and Red had spent it sleeping in a chair in the room. The first rays of dawn were just starting to show when he felt a presence in the room. Looking quickly to his right, he saw nothing until he switched into the spiritual realm. Sitting in the chair next to his was his angelic guardian!

"Hello. We haven't had proper introductions; my name is Raziel."

It was a strange feeling to be talking with an angel, but it was comforting knowing he was there.

"Hi. I guess you know my name is Red." He chuckled at this.

"Actually, your name is Redmond, but I'll call you Red if that's your preference."

"Why are you here?"

"As I said, we haven't been introduced, and you need some encouragement. I'm not just a fighter. I also give messages when necessary."

"Wow, ok. Yes, I could use something to pick me up."

"You're not responsible for Sammy's choices. I told you before, but it's something you need to accept. He could have chosen to join Buster's group of gunmen, but he didn't. He chose to warn all of you. Just as he chose to do the right thing in that situation, separate from you, he's also chosen the wrong path at times, also separate from you."

"I know he has freedom to choose, but I influenced him heavily in the past. Now he came to warn all of us and got seriously injured."

Raziel could see this man needed a little more to understand the message fully. He laid his right hand on the shoulder of the distraught man and said one word.

"Peace."

Red felt something indescribable flow into him—a calmness beyond his understanding. He felt his mind affected by this sudden stillness. He was able to clearly understand that Sammy was the decision maker for himself, and he stopped struggling with it.

It was good to have a heavenly helper.

THIRTY-ONE

February 2, 2009

I t had been just over a year since the night they were pushed off the road. Al and the detective were finally cleared to return to their jobs. Both had sustained serious injuries from the car falling down that small cliff. An investigation into who had pushed them hadn't turned up anything. It seemed as if the vehicle had disappeared without a trace, along with the driver.

Both of them were foggy about the conversation they had that night. They knew they'd discovered something important, but neither of them could remember what that was. To make matters worse, Whitaker's notebook had been lost in the crash. It was frustrating to both men, and the doctors had instructed them not to push too hard mentally.

"It may come in time, or it may never come at all. Just let your mind heal as well as your body."

Easier said than done.

Captain Dahlstrom called both of them into his office immediately.

"Good to see the two of you back. How are you feeling?"

Both men admitted they were still a little stiff and sore but that they eagerly wanted to work. The boredom of sitting at home for a year had taken its toll, and they wanted to find who'd done this to them.

"We've left the case open, and every member of this force knows to report anything that may connect to it." The captain continued. "Just get back to the usual routine of work and we'll figure this out."

With that, Dahlstrom dismissed the two and they began their first day back, determined to find answers.

THIRTY-TWO

Present Day

S ammy had woken up a little. He was mostly incoherent, but being conscious was a good sign. Red heard him try to ask if anyone else got hurt, and he reassured him that no one had. He knew the young man had heard him, as a smile appeared on his face just before he lost consciousness again.

At that point, the same nurse from the waiting room came in to check on her patient. She looked very surprised to see Red there and vocalized this.

"Oh, I didn't think any of you Christians had cared enough to stay."

"I've been here the whole time. He's sort of a prodigy of mine, and I felt a bit responsible for him being here." Red looked a bit ashamed and added, "It's a long story."

"Well, I need to do some checks on him, so you'll have to leave for that." She paused and then added, "But from what the monitors are showing me, he seems very stable." Red was relieved to hear her say that and he thanked her.

Just as he was about to exit the emergency department, Al walked in.

"So is he gonna be ok?"

Red updated him on what the nurse had just told him and they left the hospital together. Suddenly, Red realized that he hadn't eaten all night and that he'd left Scarlett at the church.

"Hey, I need a ride and some food. Murphy's?"

Al quickly agreed and they climbed into Old Blue for the trip.

"I had a conversation with Raziel last night."

Al looked confused at this.

"My 'heavenly helper,' as I like to call … him? Not sure how that works with angels." They both laughed at this and then got more serious. "It was interesting. I still haven't gotten used to angels being a real thing, never mind having conversations with them."

Al agreed. "Yeah, it's weird for sure. Jeremy never explained that part to us. I wonder if he knew." They both sat in silent nostalgic reflection for a few minutes until they arrived at Murphy's.

After their meal, they went to Harmony to pick up Scarlett. Some of the church members had rolled her into an alcove at the back of the building to keep her safe. Red expressed his gratitude to them, and a senior man spoke to him about the quality of work put into her.

"She's a beauty for sure, great workmanship, but you might want to change that." He pointed at the scantily clad woman on top of the tank.

"Yeah, I really should get on that; thanks for reminding me."

The older man responded with a knowing wink and a smile. As Red rode away, he realized that even the older Christians had a past. No one was perfect.

THIRTY-THREE

June 4, 2011

ason Satanovic was proud of his latest death vehicle—
that's what he called them. It was perfect for the task.
A large 4x4 pickup, he had reinforced the grille with
heavy steel and put a skid plate in to prevent damage. He'd
found some barely used offroad tires in the yard, and even
some headlight shields.

Satan had visited him and commanded him to build
a tough vehicle for a special purpose. It had taken him
two weeks but it was finally finished, and he awaited his
master's instruction.

He thought about the day Satan had first revealed himself, now almost forty years ago. He'd just turned eighteen,
and it was also the day his father had died. Satan knew
Jason had been beaten and otherwise abused by his earthly
father. He told Jason that he'd killed his father so that he
could be a good father-figure to him. These were all lies,
of course, but the poorly treated young man had no idea.

He remembered inheriting the large vehicle recycling facility once the investigation into his father's death was finished. He'd worked hard for the first two years, keeping it going and getting the finances in better order. It was at this point that Satan had come back, promising to give him riches and power and freedom. He just wanted him to kill certain people now and then.

At first Jason was aghast. *How can I murder anyone, even for all of those things?* He initially refused, but suddenly business stopped. No one was coming to him, and the bills were soon past due. So when Satan came back, he accepted the first assignment, albeit hesitantly. Afterwards, he threw up violently and Satan laughed at this, calling him a "terrestrial being." True to his word, however, he led Jason to a vehicle in the yard and told him to look in the spare tire well. When he examined it, he found a large amount of cash wadded up inside of an old sock!

After this, Jason did Satan's bidding whenever he asked, and there was always some major payment provided. He even began to worship the evil spiritual being; the more he worshipped, the more he was rewarded.

Suddenly, the evil being appeared and examined the truck.

"Well done, my servant, well done indeed. This will work."

THIRTY-FOUR
Present Day

Red had taken possession of Sammy's bike after the police were finished with it. He and Ben had picked it up with Ben's truck, and now it sat in the garage at the Den. It was riddled with holes from the bullets that had passed through it from the shooting at the church.

The two men noted that it needed a new tank, one fender, the seat, a couple of lights, and some mechanical parts. The engine block had cracked from a direct hit, and some of the side covers had holes in them as well.

Sighing deeply, they made a long list of the parts needed after they'd disassembled it and realized that they didn't have everything. They took stock of what parts they did have, and after reviewing what they didn't have, Red began to think of where they could obtain the missing pieces. He suddenly remembered that Dalberton Vehicle Recycling took motorcycles as well as cars and trucks. It was mid-afternoon, so he knew they had time.

He and Ben drove over there in his pickup to search for the missing pieces.

As they entered the office, both of them had an uneasy feeling about the place, but they didn't know why. They would before they left.

The owner directed them to the appropriate section of the yard for bikes while giving them both a strange look. After getting most of the parts they needed, they were looking around for any more bikes when Red noticed one partially hidden in a building. They went in through the open end of the structure and had to find their way past various vehicle parts and pieces.

After getting to the bike, they found the part they needed and quickly removed it. Looking around the inside of this building, they noticed two vehicles at the back. They were both covered with tarps, and the men's curiosity got the better of them. Glancing towards the open end of the building to make sure no one was coming, they lifted the corner of the tarp on the car.

What they saw made Red go completely white.

Under the tarp was a black car with heavy steel bracing welded to it!

They pulled back the corner of the other tarp to reveal a large 4x4 pickup, again with heavy steel reinforcement. When Ben examined the bumper area, he went pale. It had bright green paint all over it from an impact with another vehicle!

Nancy's car had been bright green—the exact shade on this truck!

THIRTY-FIVE

June 5, 2011

Nancy Parsons was on her way to Harmony Fellowship Church. She was singing along with the Christian radio station as she drove. She was happy at the thought of becoming a mother, and her husband was a good man. Although she still hadn't convinced him to come to church with her, she wasn't going to let that get her down this morning.

She came to a four-way stop, and after seeing that the truck to her left had not yet stopped, she continued on. With no warning, the 4x4 accelerated towards her at the quickest speed possible!

The large truck hit the driver's door of the bright green compact car hard, destroying the entire side of it. Nancy was killed instantly.

The truck driver backed up and sped away, smiling.

Satan was laughing as he "rode" in the passenger side.

THiRTY-SiX

Present Day

Red and Ben both had to work hard to gather their composure. Thankfully, Nathaniel and Raziel had come to comfort them. After their nerves settled, they went to the counter to pay for the parts and left without saying a word. After they left the salvage yard, they looked at each other in shocked amazement.

"He's the serial killer!" They exclaimed in unison.

Another pause and Red continued.

"We need to tell Al what we found."

Ben agreed and they drove straight to the police station.

Detective Whitaker was at his desk, but Al was out on patrol, so they spoke with the detective. When they told him what they'd found, the experienced man sent a notification out for all available units to meet at the junkyard. He then quickly went into the captain's office without knocking and informed him of what they'd found.

The captain got on the phone immediately and let the chief know that he was issuing an emergency search warrant for the recycling compound. Knowing the importance of being swift, Whitaker told Red and Ben to ride with him but to stay out of the way when they arrived.

As the police were walking into the yard, they heard the sound of the vehicle crusher starting up. They rushed in with guns drawn and saw Jason beginning to crush the pickup truck; he also had a gun, which he quickly turned on the police. Whitaker crouched behind a junked car, and Satanovic turned to fire at a junior officer who hadn't gotten behind anything in time.

As Satanovic aimed at the junior officer, Whitaker raised himself up just high enough and fired one shot, killing the murderer instantly. Another officer confirmed that he was dead and quickly shut off the crusher before the evidence was destroyed.

During the investigation, they discovered a shrine to Satan and photos of some of the accident scenes, including Whitaker and Al's. They also discovered a log of dates and times, along with roads and number of victims, male and female. When all of this was recorded and collected, it was clear that Jason Satanovic had been the serial killer they'd been looking for.

THIRTY-SEVEN
June 5, 2011

The detective was deeply troubled by this latest hit and run death. The scene was gruesome—a young pregnant woman crushed inside her small car. Examining the scene, he found some important details, such as many areas where the bright green paint had obviously transferred to the other vehicle. Also, it was clear that whatever had hit this little car had done so on purpose, as indicated by the rubber on the road from acceleration.

Other than those small bits of evidence, there was nothing else to glean from the scene. He again felt frustrated because he truly believed this was the work of that same killer. Now he had the exceptionally unpleasant task of informing this young lady's husband that she was gone.

THIRTY-EIGHT

Present Day

Red and Ben had gone to the police station to fill out proper statements about the discovery of the murder vehicles. It had taken longer than they expected, but at the end of it all, Captain Dahlstrom thanked the men for what he called a "huge help" in the case.

Al finished his shift while they were giving their reports and he met them afterwards at the biker Den to talk about what had transpired that day. Marvelling at the details, he was also very thankful that they had finally found Jeremy's killer.

The three men wept openly from the emotional strain of it all, each of them having faced personal loss at the hands of Jason Satanovic. They unloaded the parts for Sammy's bike, then said their goodbyes. Ben drove off in his truck. Al and Red both realized that they hadn't eaten for a while, so they agreed to meet at Murphy's.

Red headed out on Scarlett while Al was getting into Old Blue. He was about to put her in gear when he saw a familiar face in a beat-up pickup truck follow Red down the road.

Buster.

Knowing this could turn out badly, he quickly called into the station to request assistance with a suspect in the shootings at the church. Having been assured that officers were on their way, he discreetly followed the dangerous man.

Buster followed Red down several roads and then turned off onto a side street. This caused Al to feel as if he was wrong about Buster's intentions. Continuing to follow the bad biker, he realized too late what the evil man had planned when he remembered that the side street actually intersected the road Red had taken.

Red rode straight into the intersection, as he had the right of way, but he didn't see the large pickup as it barrelled down on him. The impact almost made Al throw up, but he kept his fear for his friend under control, knowing Buster wasn't finished.

Al quickly pulled Old Blue to the edge of the road and got out, running to Red and fearing the worst. Red was lying separate from Scarlett. His left leg was a mangled mess, but he was alive. Realizing that Buster had also stopped his truck, Al turned to see a gun aimed at Red. Buster didn't seem to notice Al but was screaming at Red while sirens blared a short distance away.

"I should have done this when I took care of Larry and that brat kid of his. You *never* should have been the leader. I worked for that for years!"

It was obvious that the mention of Larry and Logan made an impact on Red.

"Yeah, that's right, I killed them in that alley the night he named you as the new leader. He should've known better, and you should have too. Messing with me was the biggest mistake of your life, kid."

He raised the gun quickly, but Al had anticipated this, moving in front of his injured friend. The shot meant for Red hit Al in the abdomen, and suddenly another shot rang out. Buster's face drained of all colour just before he fell dead to the earth.

THIRTY-NINE

July 18, 2013

Harold Ontager was alone praying in Harmony Fellowship Church. He had felt moved by the Holy Spirit to do so, but he wasn't sure who or what he was supposed to be praying about. He was an experienced Christian, however, so he just began to pray. He knew that the Lord would give the answers he needed.

After he said "Amen," he looked up and saw his angelic guardian standing before him.

"Hello, Harold." A grin from the celestial being was followed by a serious look.

"Hello again, my old companion." He always enjoyed these moments.

"You'll be needed soon. There's a young man on the brink of destruction who will need your help."

"How will I know who this young man is?"

"It will be made clear to you. *Don't* ignore the call when it comes."

FORTY

Present Day

Red had been in the hospital for two weeks and was finally able to walk on crutches, so he was released. Ben and Devin had informed him that the shot Al had blocked was fatal. His lifelong friend was dead. Red was reeling from the news of Al's death, but he knew he was with the Lord and Jeremy.

He wasn't sure what to do now; his life had been changed so dramatically. The doctors had been able to save his leg, but it was full of pins and even a couple of plates. They said he'd never be able to ride a bike again; shifting was done by his left leg, and it wasn't able to make the motions anymore. That part didn't matter much at this point, as Scarlett had been bent almost in half by the impact and couldn't be salvaged.

Ben met him in the waiting room to give him a ride to Al's funeral; they had delayed it by a week to allow him to attend. Red was amazed at the turnout when they got to the gravesite. While he prayed for strength, he looked at his oldest friend in the casket and saw an amazing sight.

Al was fully armoured, with his sword lying lengthwise on his chest, and his shield on top of it. He had a smile on his face, and Red knew he was happy and at peace. This caused Red to feel great joy about his friend.

A month later, his leg was doing much better when he had a visitor at the Den. A lawyer showed up asking for him by his full name, and Red grew concerned that this might be something bad. Surprisingly, however, the man had come to get him to sign some documents about Al's will. After signing the papers, the man handed him the keys to Old Blue. Al had arranged this in his will decades ago while they were still at odds with each other.

Red wept out of joy.

He got a taxi to his friend's home and found Old Blue in the driveway, ready for him to take her to her new home. He got in and fired up the large V8, remembering all of the times he'd sat in the passenger side. He shifted into drive and marvelled at how happy he felt driving this classic machine.

While he drove down the road, an old familiar song came to his memory.

"He is the way, He is the truth, He is the liiiiife! That's Jesus!"

EPİLOGUE

THAT'S JESUS!

He is the way, He is the truth, He is the liiiiife!
That's Jesus!

You are the way, you are the truth, you are the liiiiife!
Lord Jesus!

He is the way, He is the truth, He is the liiiiife!
My Jesus!

WARRIOR OF LIGHT

Ben Parsons' grief over tragedy has brought him to a dead-end. Then a wrong-number call shows him the spiritual side of life and that there is another road to take.

EVANGELIST OF LIGHT

Charged with supernatural intensity, this inspiring novel is both an engaging story of perseverance and a deep exploration of faith.